The Boy in the Smoke

The Boy in the Smoke

A SHADES OF LONDON BOOK

MAUREEN JOHNSON

HOT
KEY
BOOKS

First published in Great Britain in 2014 by Hot Key Books
Northburgh House, 10 Northburgh Street, London EC1V 0AT

A CIP catalogue record for this book is available from the British Library.

ISBN: 978-1-4714-0322-4

1

This book is typeset in 10.5 Berling LT Std using Atomik ePublisher

Printed and bound by Clays Ltd, St Ives Plc

Hot Key Books supports the Forest Stewardship Council (FSC),
the leading international forest certification organisation, and is
committed to printing only on Greenpeace-approved FSC-certified paper.

www.hotkeybooks.com

Hot Key Books is part of the Bonnier Publishing Group
www.bonnierpublishing.com

I

THE FORGOTTEN BOY

You can tell when your parents dislike you—when they are horrified by the way you eat, at your bodily fluids, at the noises you make and the way you play. You know when you perpetually give them a headache or make them vanish into another room and leave you with the housekeeper or each other or the dog, whatever is handy.

Another way you can tell is when it is the last day of prep school, and they forget to come and get you and go on holiday to Barbados instead.

This is how Stephen Dene finally figured it out. He had suspected it for years, but it was just a vague, uneasy feeling. This was proof—hard, solid proof. If he had been in a courtroom drama, this was the kind of thing the Crown could have produced at the end with a major flourish.

"And do you deny, that on Friday, the 15th of May, you left your thirteen-year-old son, Stephen Dene, sitting on the front steps of Chatwick House at St. George's School, looking like a total

tit? Do you deny not answering your phones because you were at
the hotel spa the entire day being wrapped in seaweed or ginger
or some other pore-opening swill while your son was left to rot?"

And his parents would be sitting in the witness box looking
tanned and shamed. The jury would scowl at them. The judge
would look down from the bench and bore holes into the tops
of their well-groomed heads.

Stephen watched a lot of crime shows and police dramas,
so this is where his mind went in times of stress. He often
fantasized about becoming a police officer. He liked the idea
of chasing down criminals and helping people who were hurt.
It was a practical job, one that made sense. He asked his father
about it once.

"Don't be stupid," his father replied. "We're not sending
you to these kinds of schools to become a *plod*."

No. Apparently, they sent him to schools like this so he could
sit alone on his trunk in the mid-May sunshine, smelling the
first bloom of the summer, watching car after car after car leave
the school. And as the numbers grew smaller, the questioning
looks he got from those leaving became more questioning. What
was wrong with Dene? Where was his family? The numbers
dwindled. It was just him and Anderson and Dex. Dex never
even looked up from the video game he was playing when
he got into his parents' car. Anderson tried to talk to him
about football, and then they both got bored and anxious and
stared down the drive, waiting to see which car would turn
the green and shady corner first. When it was Anderson's, and
when Anderson's parents emerged frantically talking about
car trouble and apologizing and hugging him—that's when

10

Stephen felt something in him go into freefall.

His parents did not have car trouble. Of that, he was reasonably certain. He reached into his pocket to retrieve his phone to text his sister.

They forgot to get me.

The replies came quickly, one on top of the other.

????????

You're still there???

I'll kill them.

U ok?

Don't worry.

Then she sent a picture of herself making a rageful face.

When everyone else was gone, and the school grounds were creepily quiet except for the sound of birds screaming away in the trees, the headmaster's wife took Stephen inside to their private residence. She gave him a plate of cold chicken and packaged Waitrose coleslaw on a tray. Then the headmaster and his wife went into the kitchen and spoke behind a closed door, but he could hear more or less every word.

"Their housekeeper is coming," he heard the headmaster say.

"There's always one," his wife said. She was trying, and failing, to keep her voice low. "It's always so sad. I wonder why these people have children? And such a shame it's Dene. He's a lovely boy. So smart. Going to Eton. And . . ."

They must have gone further from the door, or realized they were speaking too loudly, because all Stephen heard from this point on was a mumble.

He pulled out his phone again.

Paulina is coming to get me, he texted. **Don't worry**.

His sister's reply came within seconds.

Vengeance!!!! I love you.

Two hours later, Paulina, their housekeeper, pulled up in her car. Her job was to clean the house twice a week, not to drive all the way to the outskirts of Cheltenham to pick up forgotten children. Paulina's English was poor, and she had little to say to Stephen or the people at the school. She was always kind, though, and greeted him with a Twix bar and a sympathetic manner. Stephen tried to make some conversation on the drive back. He didn't really speak Polish, but had taken the first two levels of an online, self-teaching course in order to try to communicate with her. She always appreciated his efforts and smiled, though it was a wincing smile that suggested he was destroying her language with the dull edge of his tongue.

So it was a long, quiet trip.

When they arrived at the house a few hours later, there was already music playing from an upstairs room. Only one person in the Dene household played music out loud, and it was the only person Stephen wanted to see. It was also the only person who *shouldn't* have been there. That person came running down the stairs in bare feet, wearing a short blue dress and silver bangles halfway up her arms.

"Stephen!"

Regina ran directly to him, wrapping her arms around him tightly. Though his sister was three years older, she was also seven inches shorter. Stephen had grown fast—at thirteen he was closing in on six feet. Gina had remained a tiny terror with a whip of dark brown hair.

"Why are you here?" Stephen asked, when she let him go.

"Hello to you too."

"I mean . . . don't you have a few days left of term?"

"There was no way I was going to let you be all alone. I left."

"Left? What about your exams?"

"What's more important, exams or *you*?"

"Your exams?" Stephen said.

"No." Gina sat primly on the stairs. "*You* are more important."

The fact that she had skipped her exams meant that Gina would very likely be expelled from her third school. Stephen turned this news around in his mind for a moment, then deliberately tried to let it go and not worry. This attempt failed.

This was the arrangement in the Dene household: Gina was the troubled one, and Stephen was the good one. These were the roles assigned at birth. Stephen was the one who could easily have sailed through school without making much of an effort, but he was the kind of person who couldn't really help but make an effort and so was regarded as exceptional and 'a good boy' more or less everywhere he went. That he had been accepted to Eton only cemented this status. Which still wasn't enough for his parents to remember he existed.

And Gina, the bad one, was the one who did all the good things, like made sure Stephen had someone to come home to. She had absolutely no fear—not of their parents, of authority, of the future, of heights, spiders, the dark . . . When she came into a room, that room was illuminated and doubts dismissed. She had to know she was about to be expelled, and yet here she was on the stairs, looking bright-eyed and playing with her bangles.

13

Why it had turned out this way, he never knew. This would be like asking why the stars had adopted their particular positions in the sky.

"*They* called, by the way," Regina said. "They said they can't get back until Monday. *Can't get back*. I suppose they've been taken prisoner. So it's you and me for a few days! What do you want to do? Want to go to Spain?"

"Spain?"

"Sure. We could be there tonight, if you want."

"Didn't they take your credit card?" Stephen asked.

"They put a limit on it, but I just sorted that out."

"How?"

"I texted them and told them to up my limit or I'd call child services for neglect. We couldn't make a case for it, but a social worker would have to come around and ask questions. I told them ten thousand would do it. How about Paris? Let's have a *proper weekend*, you and me."

To be honest, Stephen was a little scared of Gina's idea of a proper weekend—but once again, there was something in his sister's delivery that made it all right.

"I don't know . . . London?" he said. "We could stay at Dad's flat?"

"Don't you want to do something bigger than that?"

London was hardly a journey. They lived in Kent, only forty minutes on the train. But Stephen rarely got to go there.

"All right." Regina nodded. She looked maybe a little disappointed that they wouldn't be going further afield, but was prepared to accept it. "London it is. Go change and pack. We leave in an hour."

An hour later, Stephen and Regina got in a taxi to the train station—which was a quick enough walk, but there were bags, and Gina didn't walk with bags. Paulina was confused, and Stephen attempted to lie and say that their parents had called and they were supposed to meet them in London. Stephen couldn't really lie in English, so lying in Polish was never really going to work. Paulina looked concerned but had no power to stop them. Plus, she trusted Stephen, so he felt like a bit of a villain lying to her.

"This is your weekend," Gina said, once they were on the train. "We're going to do whatever *you* want."

"You'd be bored," Stephen said. This was undeniably true. Stephen's tastes tended to run to museums, bookshops and comic stores. Also, he really would have been happy just sitting around and watching television, reading, playing video games and eating crisps for two days. That would have suited him just fine.

"Whatever *you* want," Gina said again spreading her arms wide.

Stephen would later remember the following two days as two of the best in his life. The flat was in Maida Vale, which was well located for the shops that Gina loved to frequent. They walked down to Oxford Street (more shops, more of Gina picking out clothes for herself and Stephen), then down to Soho, which Stephen experienced through an endless sequence of coffees. Gina bought a vintage dress and danced down the middle of the street. She indulged Stephen in Charing Cross as he worked his way through all the bookstores.

Mostly, though, they talked. Gina was probably the only person Stephen actually talked to. You could say absolutely anything to Gina. She didn't judge. You didn't have to be clever. And she was actually interested—or at least seemed to be—in what he was doing. With everyone else, he was Stephen Dene, the good and sensible son and student. Only Gina brought out the rest.

On Sunday afternoon, they went to an American-style diner just off of Piccadilly, and they both ordered far too much food—oversized burgers, chips, milkshakes. The food spilled off the plates, but they ate it all.

"A friend of mine is going to come by while we're here," Gina said. "Just for a second."

"Who?"

"Just a friend," Gina said, smiling.

"A friend from London?"

"From my last school," Gina said. "She just texted. She'll be here in a minute. She won't stay long."

There was something in the way Gina was fidgeting and looking down at her plate that told Stephen there was something about this friend—something Gina didn't want to say.

"What's she coming for?"

"Just to give me something," Gina said, with a smile. "Something I left at her flat."

A few minutes later a tall blonde girl came in and tapped Gina on the back of her head.

"Heya!" Gina bounded from her seat. "Julianne, this is Stephen, my brother."

"The Eton one, yeah?" Julianne said.

16

"I only have the one. We'll be right back, Stephen. Don't eat all my chips."

The two excused themselves and went to the women's toilets. He watched them hustle to the back, their heads together. Julianne clutched her purse like a rugby ball. They were gone for about ten minutes, and Gina returned alone, with a wide smile. She bounced back into her seat and started grabbing some chips.

"What was that?" he asked.

"Oh, nothing."

"Come on. Just tell me. I'm not an idiot."

She laughed and took some whipped cream from her milkshake and swiped at his nose. Her pupils were huge.

Gina was very chatty that long afternoon—and she remained that way until the phone rang when they were back in the flat. From the way her face fell, Stephen knew it had to be their parents.

"Why aren't *you* at home?" Gina said. "Oh? Well, maybe Paulina is lying. We're upstairs."

From his spot on the sofa, Stephen watched this conversation with unease.

"Oh . . . I do. I feel *terrible*. I feel so bad. I hope you got a tan, at least. And you're . . ." She looked at the phone and shrugged.

"They're coming back," Gina said, tossing the phone on to the floor, where it clattered and spun. She walked across the room and half-climbed into the drinks cabinet, emerging with a bottle of whiskey.

"This looks expensive," she said. "But I hate single malt."

She opened the bottle and poured the contents into a potted palm, then took out a bottle of vodka instead. She poured some of this into a tall crystal glass and raised it as if making a toast.

"They know we're not at home," Stephen said.

"They know."

"They're angry."

Gina shrugged and sipped.

"When are they going to be here?"

"Tonight," she said. "They're getting on a plane now."

"Are we supposed to go home? What's happening?"

Gina got up and started circling the living room with the strange, slow focus of a lazy bee—she was definitely thinking something, but what that thing was, Stephen had no idea. Something was building inside of her. He could see it in her eyes and restless circling and the way she played with her bracelets.

"You can't go to Eton," she said.

Stephen didn't answer this, because this wasn't something that required a reply. He was going to go to Eton in the same way that the sun was going to rise in the morning and gravity would continue to bind them to the earth. Getting into Eton was the single biggest achievement of his life.

"I mean it," she said. "You can't go. I have to stop it."

"What?"

"You know what it's like there," she said.

"It's just school."

"It's not just school and you know it."

Stephen actually did know what she meant. Eton produced Society's Monsters—everyone knew that. Politicians, mostly, and occasionally people who ran banks and all the other institutions

18

that stole the world's spoils for themselves. Every once in a while Eton produced someone who made up for it a little—an actor, usually. Maybe a scientist. Usually an actor. Stephen couldn't act, so he saw no particular hope in that direction. By going, he might easily join a line of privileged, heartless people who thought the world was a system to be owned, to be beaten, to be won.

It was also the best. Everyone knew that too. And Stephen was competitive. Many people from his school had sat the Eton entrance exam. He was the only one who'd made it.

"You're so good," Gina said. There was a sleepiness to her voice. A sad, dreamy quality. "You're so good. You'd do anything for anyone. They don't deserve you. None of them."

In a completely unexpected move, she made a sudden pounce at the wall and attached herself to one of the heavy floor-length curtains. She was slight enough that she could hang from it for a moment even with her full weight on it.

"Gina, what are you . . ."

The curtain rod pulled free of the wall and the curtain crumpled to the floor, landing like an injured ballerina.

"Know how much these curtains cost?" Gina said. "Mum told me. They cost five grand apiece."

She wrapped herself around the next curtain, and Stephen felt his fear building. He had seen Gina get erratic before, but this was a new level.

"You don't need to do this," he said. "They're just curtains."

"They forgot you," Gina said. The second curtain fell to the ground, along with the rod it hung from. She stood up and walked to the desk, where she got a large pair of scissors.

19

"Gina . . ."

"Stephen," she said, sounding very calm, "they forgot you. I need to help them arrange their priorities. You are more important than these curtains."

She used the scissors to point at the curtains.

"I understand, but . . ."

Gina got to the floor and began to cut away at the fabric. Stephen sat down on the edge of the sofa and nervously watched her make ribbons out of the material. The curtains were heavy, so she had to chop hard. Unsure of what to do, he turned to the television and flipped through the channels until he found a police show he knew on one of the constant repeat channels. He put it on mute and watched it for a moment to steady himself. When he turned back to Gina, he realized she was crying. This sent a new wave of panic through his system. He got up and crouched near her, then sat down on the edge of the curtain and put a tentative arm around her shoulder. She continued to cut the curtain as if nothing was happening.

"I have a plan," she said. "Would you like to hear it?"

He nodded, albeit a bit warily.

"I'm sixteen now, so I could leave school, but Mum promised that if I made it through this year without any trouble, they'd get me a flat in London."

"You're joking."

"I'm not. They know I'm never going to university, so they're going to have to make some provisions now. In fact, they've already looked at a few places. It's an investment, right? You know they love buying property."

"But you just left school without taking any exams."

"I got close enough," she said. "And anything to get me out of the house. It probably won't be an expensive flat, but it will be enough. It'll be in London. I have friends here. This is where I want to be. As soon as I have that flat, I'm coming for you. You'll come and live with me."

"And just leave school?"

"You can go to school in London. There are loads of comprehensives in London. I'm going to get a job at somewhere cool like Vivienne Westwood or something. And you'll live with me, and neither one of us will ever go home again."

This was madness. This plan had no relationship with reality. It was possible that after a few glasses of wine his parents had told Gina that if she got through the year they'd get her a flat. They said things like that sometimes, but they never meant them. And even if they had, they certainly wouldn't buy her one after she ran away on the eve of her exams. There was no flat. There would be no running away from Eton and living together. Gina said crazy things sometimes, but not like this. Not seriously—not like she really meant it.

"You just can't go to Eton," Gina said calmly, still cutting away. "It's my job to save you. So we'll live in the flat."

"There's nothing to save me from," Stephen said. "Whatever you think they'll turn me into, they won't."

"You won't be able to help it."

"Yes, I will. Don't you trust me?"

At that, Gina started sobbing properly. She threw her arms around his neck and held him close. He felt her heart beating wildly against his chest and had no idea what to say to make her stop crying. So he just sat there with her until she calmed down and detached herself.

"I have a bit more to do," she said, getting up and wiping at her eyes. "They'll be here in a few hours."

She went into the kitchen, and Stephen heard the sound of glasses being dropped, one by one, on to the floor. He got up and went into the kitchen and watched her break every bit of glassware and crockery in the room, including a complete set of Viennese crystal and bone china. He could have stopped her—he was bigger and stronger—but he would not touch her.

He'd never felt so helpless.

When she was done with that, she took a steak knife and tore apart the fabric in one of the sofas until the stuffing popped out of the slashes. She seemed satisfied with that and dropped the knife.

"I'm going to take a nap now," she said. She did look drowsy, her eyes at half-mast. "Wake me when Mater and Pater arrive."

Stephen looked at the scene of destruction around him. Gina had said they were getting on a plane now, but it wasn't clear where the plane was from—Barbados, a connecting airport? His time window was a few hours, enough to sweep up the glass and throw away the shredded curtains. Nothing could replace the curtains or fix the sofa. He did what he could. He tried to put the rails back up, but they'd been ripped from the walls and the screws had bent and left gaping holes. He swept up the glass and closed all the now-empty cabinets. He flipped the sofa cushions.

Then he sat and waited for the inevitable.

His parents arrived just after midnight. They were very tanned. There were no hugs. The two of them came in and surveyed the room.

"Where's your sister?" his mother asked.

"Asleep. I did this. All of it."

"No you didn't," his father said. "Be quiet."

In reply, Stephen reached out and slapped a vase right off a table. It landed on the wooden floor and broke fairly cleanly into a few large pieces. He would have preferred a grand shatter, but this would have to do.

Gina laughed and clapped from the doorway of the bedroom. She had woken up.

"Shut *up*, Regina," their mother said. "You know you did this. Whatever it is, it's always you. Stephen is just trying to protect you and is making a fool out of himself. Do you want to ruin everything and make your brother into a fool?"

"Stephen is the only one of us that isn't a fool," Gina said. "And you *left* him at school."

"Stop being dramatic."

"Does 'dramatic' mean saying what actually happened?" Gina replied. "I'm going to make sure everyone knows you forgot him. Everyone will know what utter, utter tossers you are."

"Stephen," his father said. "Gather up whatever you've brought. We're leaving."

Unsure of what else to do, Stephen obeyed. He hastily threw everything into a bag and came back to find a silent stand-off still going on. Gina remained in the bedroom doorway, smirking, arms folded.

"Stephen, go to the car," his mum said.

"Come on, Gina," Stephen said.

"I'm staying here," Gina replied.

"Not in this flat, you're not," his father said. "You'll leave this flat, but you're also not riding home with us. Here."

He dropped twenty pounds on the floor.

"That will get you a ticket home. Your cards are cancelled."

"Oh, you think that's scary?" Gina asked. "Making me take the train?"

But Stephen knew whatever was coming next was much worse than Gina simply taking the train. He saw it in his parents' faces. When you spend your life watching other people fighting, you learn the language of the silences and the pauses, because that's where all the really terrible decisions are made.

In the silence that followed Gina's statement, Stephen knew that something particularly bad was coming. When you live with a bomb, you should know that at some point it will go off.

"You think you're making a statement," Stephen's dad said, utterly calm. "Let me clarify. You're sixteen now. We're not paying for any more school, or anything else for that matter. You are not our problem. We'll see you at home, or we won't. Preferably the later. Come along, Stephen. Go to the car. Now."

At first, Gina laughed. Stephen almost staggered. He mentally begged her to apologize, but Gina would never do that. She kept her chin up and nodded to him, letting him know it was all right—he could go.

He should do something. Yell. Stay with Gina. Anything.

But if he did anything, said anything, he'd only make it worse. He looked to her, and it felt like the earth was ripping open between them. Why did Gina look like she'd won? What was wrong with *all of them*?

He went to the car.

Gina never came home. She moved in with some friends in a flat in Shoreditch. Later, she would tell Stephen that their parents sent her a small sum every month just to ensure that she would stay away, enough for a flatshare and some groceries. She would phone, but the calls were erratically timed—weeks of silence followed by a two a.m. call. There were lots of largely incomprehensible texts. The house was filled with pictures of Stephen in his Eton uniform, and all those of Gina were removed. In the autumn, Stephen was shipped off to start his new life.

At the time, he believed things had gotten as bad as they ever could. He was wrong.

II

THE BREAK IN THE CHAIN

Most of Stephen's life at Eton was spent running, often physically. The days started with a 7:30 breakfast, then chapel, then a sequence of divs—the Eton way of saying classes— then lunch, then sport, then more divs, then study. Very little time was provided to get from place to place, and the school sprawled for two miles, so he ran. Everyone ran. It was like a constant relay. You left your books between railings in town, in pigeonholes, on steps, and as you raced past, you picked up one set and dropped another. The entire town was littered with stacks of them. Maths to Latin to German to Divinity to Geography to French to History . . .

If you were late (and you couldn't help but be late sometimes), there was always a price to pay. The beaks always had something ready to go. Maybe a hundred lines of Milton to copy. Maybe a problem set or a translation. There was a brutal heartbeat about the place, a constant sense of movement and pressure. There was a reason the exams were called trials.

One Thursday in March, Stephen was moving swiftly between Latin and Geography divs when a prefect caught up with him and told him to go back to his house, immediately. He'd never been called back to his house before, and such a callback never meant anything good. It meant you'd done something seriously wrong, or something seriously wrong had happened somewhere in the world outside and the news would be dropped on you from a great height. Stephen had done nothing seriously wrong that he could think of, so something had to have happened. He went through every possibility he could think of as he ran.

The news could never have been predicted, and yet, somewhere in his mind he already knew it had to do with her. The universe would never be so kind as to spare her, the only one of them that was worth anything.

The Master was nice enough. Stephen was taken into the family living room and sat on the floral sofa, and the news was said gently, but with an unequivocal tone—"*your sister . . . overdose, it seems . . . nothing could be done . . .*"

Overdose, it seems.

For the first minute, those words echoed in his head. What killed Gina? Overdose, it seems. It *seems* that way, as if it might have been something else, like malaria or bad vapours or dragons, but it was an overdose, it seems. There was a roaring in his ears that obliterated all other noise. He spoke to his parents briefly on the phone, right there, in the sitting room. His mother sounded like she was crying. His father did not. If anything, he sounded angry. Stephen was given the option of going home for a bit, which he decided not to take. There was no point in going home now. After that, he was permitted to return to his room or speak to someone at the San. He went outside instead and walked up and down the high street. He had no thoughts—nothing he could remember later. His mind was a void. All he could do was walk. One of the prefects came to find him and bring him back.

Life continued, which was strange. Aside from the funeral, which took a half-day, Stephen didn't leave Eton. His parents must have been relieved, as this gave them the opportunity to work out their grief at a resort in Switzerland. Other people generally took it easy on him and the beaks were kind enough. Death, after all, was not a taboo subject at Eton—as long as it didn't get too personal. Every Etonian was constantly reminded that most people who had attended the school were, in fact, dead. When your school is almost six hundred years old, this is inevitable. The dead were all over the place—in statues and in the hundreds of portraits that bore down their gazes from every wall. Their names were etched onto every possible surface.

So for the first few weeks, there were allowances. The beaks tended to let it slip if he was a minute or two late. The Master and the Dame looked in on him, and he was always encouraged to go to the counsellor, and he always said he would think about it. One night he accidentally heard the Master say "how well Dene was getting on, after, you know, that awful business with his sister. Terrible for the family, but there's always one, isn't there? Luckily they have him."

Stephen didn't know if he was doing well. For those first days, he wasn't aware of much of anything. He opened books and closed them. He rowed. He ate some food. His body moved

28

him around until term was over. When he returned home, Gina's room was empty and had been turned into a small home exercise studio. He wandered the house, looking for anything he could find, but the culling had been complete. Her clothes, her bike, all her furniture . . . even the attic and the cellar had been cleared. The best he could do was recover several books that had wound up on the common shelves that he knew to be hers. His sister, for all her partying, loved to read. He gathered up her fantasy novels and romances and books of poetry and volumes of Shakespeare, and he put them in his closet, under a carefully constructed pile of clothes.

It turned out it had happened at a party. Gina passed out on the far side of a bed. Whatever she had taken stopped her heart almost at once, and she lay there, between the bed and the wall, for eighteen hours before someone thought to look. Stephen learned this after hearing his father relaying the story over the phone to someone. This was weeks later, when he was home for one of the short breaks in the Lent term, and his father spoke casually, as if describing an investment that didn't quite perform as hoped.

It was an image he couldn't get out of his head—Gina stuck between the bed and the wall while the party went on. He saw it when he closed his eyes at night. Sometimes he would dream about seeing a bed, hearing her voice calling to him from the space just beyond the bed, asking him for help, and he'd wake up with his heart pounding. He'd get up and open his window and stick out his head and breathe in as much cold air as he could and try to understand how there could be a world without Gina. How was it that the trees hadn't died? How was it that anything continued on? How did he continue to live? It seemed wrong and unnatural, and it would take great effort to calm down and get himself back to bed, to refocus. There was no time for grief. No time to curl into a ball and remain motionless for days. No time to explain to everyone that the world was now broken.

He often had the impulse to go and find the flat this had happened in and burn it to the ground.

In many ways, he appreciated the gruelling schedule for keeping him sane. Eton would push him forward. Onward, onward, onward. The school that seemed so fanatically rooted in the past wanted him to just move on. He progressed through Eton, keeping his head down and his marks up. He became a member of Sixth Form Select and had silver buttons on his waistcoat. He took several prizes in Latin and History, and became a very good boatman—not good enough to be in the Eight, but the next tier down. He could tell that everyone regarded him as serious and sensible, if they regarded him at all. He had no desire to stand out. Being at Eton was his job, and he intended to do it. He didn't have very much fun—he wasn't social. This was fine, as he regarded the most sociable and striving people at Eton to be a pack of sociopaths, doomed for parliament.

Everyone, of course, had their own secret interest hidden behind the closed doors of his room. Stephen still watched his police shows. It was less of a fun pastime now and more of a compulsion. The ones about real police were best, and he didn't care what they were doing. They could be chasing a murderer or dealing with a noise complaint. He just liked how useful it was, how simple and clear.

On good days, he kept the shows on in the background, often on mute, while he revised. On the bad days, he thought about chucking it all in and joining the force. The force itself might accept him. He could pass any exam they put in front of him. But the people who actually worked that job would laugh him away. Eton? What did someone from *Eton* know about normal people and dealing with things like broken windows and chasing down some drunken teenager who had a knife in a shopping plaza?

He'd probably end up behind a desk.

So he applied to Cambridge. He had no particular idea what he wanted to study, but he applied for English Literature and got in. This was enough to enrage his father for several weeks. Still, he could go into banking yet with that, so the matter was forgotten.

So it went, until the very end of Stephen's last year at Eton. It was the Fourth of June, which at Eton was the name of a holiday, and often not actually on the fourth of June. This was the largest celebration of the school year. The grounds were manicured, chairs set out, everything polished and practised and prepared for the show—that's what it was, a show. This was when everything Eton did was put on display. Speeches, art, music, prowess. Families came and had picnics and admired their fine Eton boys.

As a boatman, Stephen had a special role to play, as the boats were an integral part of the Fourth of June. Boatmen wore large boater hats all day, which would be decorated with flowers purchased from vendors who came out solely for this purpose.

So all through the morning Stephen had what amounted to a small flower shop on his head. This, as so many Eton things were, was one of those unlikely badges of honor. A hat full of flowers, checked trousers, silver buttons on your waistcoat, winged collars, bow ties . . . everything signified who you were and, more importantly, why you were better.

His parents came, which did not surprise him. The Fourth of June was when you showed up to preen and see what your money got you. They brought a hamper of champagne and a cold lunch and an oversized blanket to sit on the lawn by the river. After lunch came the Procession of Boats—one of the major events of the day, and the reason for the large hat of flowers. This was when ten boats would be rowed by ten groups of eight, with every member wearing nineteenth-century naval attire (and the hat with the flowers). As each boat passed in front of the spectators, the crews would have to stand up—a tricky business, as the boats were extremely unsteady at the best of times—and take off their hats in salute. Of course the Eton Boating Song was sung:

> *Rugby may be more clever,*
>
> *Harrow may make more row,*
>
> *But we'll row for ever,*
>
> *Steady from stroke to bow,*
>
> *And nothing in life shall sever,*

Those lines tended to go through his head a lot as he pumped away, pressing the oars back into the water, staying so carefully in rhythm. They were just, perhaps, a little too on the nose.

What everyone on the lawn wanted to see, of course, was one of the boats tip over as the boys inside stood to attention. If one started to fall, the entire boat would generally go over. This was considered the height of hilarity, boys falling into the water as they held their flower-heavy hats at their sides.

Stephen was determined not to fall, not in front of his parents. He ground his jaw as he stood, and the boat wobbled under him. Two people up, Maxwell looked very unsteady. Stephen felt the judder underneath as the boat began to wobble. There was an expectant mumble from the crowd. But Maxwell steadied, and they sat back down and rowed on.

When the show was over, Stephen rejoined his family on the lawn. His father appeared to be having some kind of informal business meeting on a neighbouring lawn blanket with some people who worked either at or with his bank. His mother was just finishing up a conversation with a few other women, and they were briefly left alone, sitting in the sun.

Maybe it was the beauty of the day. Maybe it was because, in theory, this was his day and his moment to be the object of attention. There was a gravity and import to the event. Maybe, just maybe . . .

"I want to do something for Gina," he said.

He actually had no plan to go along with this. He simply wanted to say her name. His mother tucked an empty champagne bottle back into the basket, her downturned eyes suggesting that he had done something just a bit distasteful.

"Stephen." She lowered her voice. "Not here, not today."

"If not here, where? I live here. And if not today, when?"

"I am not discussing this."

"Her. You are not discussing her."

"Correct," his mother said.

"She was your daughter," he said.

"I know perfectly well what she was. Just stop it. Stop making a scene."

Stephen looked around at the complete lack of a scene. They were still surrounded by picnics and light chatter and soft laughter and champagne and the gentle slosh of the river.

"What scene? I just wanted to talk about her. Because . . . she should have been here today."

"Why are you doing this?" his mother asked.

"Because she matters."

His mother actually rolled her eyes at this expression, and he felt himself tense. Of course, his parents wouldn't respond to a phrase like that—one that sounded like it had come right off a television programme. But Gina *did* matter and he didn't know how else to express that fact.

"Why don't you talk about her?" he said. "Don't you think we should?"

"No," his mother answered. "And I won't have today ruined. Why must you ruin everything for me?"

"*Ruin* everything? What have I *ever* ruined?"

34

He kept his voice low, but even still, one or two people turned to look. His mother stiffened. His father must have picked up on the fact that something was going on, because he concluded his conversation and rejoined them.

"Stephen," he said. "Help me get something from the car, won't you?"

They walked over the green fields to the cars. There was no one around but the attendants, and they were reasonably far back. Stephen folded his arms, expecting a minor dressing down. To his surprise, he felt a push on his shoulders that knocked him against the side of the car.

"What the hell are you doing?" his father said in a low, threatening voice.

"Talking about my sister," Stephen replied. "*Your daughter*. Remember her?"

"You always were a bit soft, weren't you? I thought they would knock that out of you here. I'll do it myself, if I have to."

Was this actually happening? Was his father threatening him, physically, here on the Eton parking grounds?

The eye-to-eye look, the stance . . . yes. This was happening. And it almost made Stephen laugh out loud. While his father probably made the occasional trip to the office gym, Stephen had spent every day of the last several years being roughed up on the rugby pitch, stuck in wall game scrums, and rowing for hours a day. He was stronger than his father now, undoubtedly much faster, and just a hair taller. He was not a fighter, but the simple nature of his sporting life meant he was used to taking and dealing with body blows, and it would hardly be a difficult matter to throw a punch that knocked his father flat to the ground.

"I'd really like to see you try," Stephen said quietly. "It would make my year."

This remark hit home. His father blinked. He hadn't expected Stephen to react this way, and now he was reassessing the situation. Stephen pushed up his sleeves.

His father stepped back a bit and shook his head.

"*Your sister* wasted her entire life," he said. "She was a destructive drug addict who got herself expelled from every school. She threw away every opportunity that was handed to her."

"And how do you think she got that way?" Stephen asked.

"I suppose you're going to try to tell me that it was somehow our fault, our fault for giving her *everything*."

"Except attention. Except . . ."

He couldn't say love. That was a step too far. But his father knew where the sentence was going and smirked.

"You were always the smart one, Stephen, except when it came to her. She had you exactly where she wanted you."

"What does *that* mean?"

"It means your sister used you to defend her, just like she used us and used everyone around her. She could always play you . . ."

"She didn't *play* me," Stephen spat.

"Didn't she?" Stephen's father leaned against the door of the car opposite. "She told you everything, didn't she? And you're not stupid. *You* knew she was taking drugs, didn't you? *You* knew she was in trouble."

Everything seemed to go quiet. Stephen could feel his pulse

heavy just behind his ear. The evidence had been circumstantial. That's the term they would have used on a police show. The behaviour problems. The meeting in the diner, with the trip to the toilets and the large pupils. The way Gina spoke on the phone sometimes—far too quickly, jumping from subject to subject, or far too slowly, getting confused mid-sentence. He had never asked because he didn't want to know. He didn't want to know because Gina had to be okay, even when she wasn't.

"Of course you did," his father went on. "You knew, and what did you do about it?"

"I was fourteen—"

"—and the only person your sister listened to. What did you do about it, Stephen?"

The question rung through the air, deafening him, like a close-range gunshot. Everything became muffled and painful. Of course, Stephen had asked himself this question—what had he done? The answer was nothing. He had reassured himself on this point for three years, but now that his father had asked the question, the bandage was ripped off and the wound was revealed and was still bleeding. A beating would have been preferable. He would have let it happen.

"You did the smart thing," his father said, in that casual tone that Stephen hated so very much. "You carried on. You looked after yourself and you did well. Now be smart and stop this nonsense and let's get back. You've done well today. Let's carry on."

Stephen followed, numb. Beaten.

His mother had him pose with the other members of his eight for photographs, and the chatter started anew, and between his friends people started murmuring their plans for later. As the day wore on—one of those endless early summer days when the sun simply never sets—the crowds thinned and the cars began to depart.

Stephen felt nothing. He was vaguely aware that it was a bit cooler. He noticed that around him people were happy. He walked back to his house because his body knew the way. He accepted two glasses of warm champagne because someone put them in his hand. But he wasn't there for any of it. Some part of him had simply switched off. Now that the Fourth of June had been done, the house was filled with music, and people wandering the halls in various stages of undress and shouting from room to room. Stephen remained as he was, in his boating uniform, flopped on his bed. He took out his phone and flicked through the photos of his sister—the ones he'd transferred onto two different phones, the ones he would never get rid of, even if they were blurry and repetitive. He had fifty-six photos of her on the phone, and he had looked at them a thousand times or more, night after night. The images were stained into his memory. These were the only fifty-six expressions in the world that meant anything.

And what did you do? Nothing.

When it was time to continue the party at the old boathouse, Stephen followed along and had a few more glasses of champagne. The party wore on and spilled out of the boathouse on to the lawn behind. People started pushing one another into the river. And when he himself was pushed in, fully dressed and glass in hand—as he sank into the dark water and sprung back to the surface—he accepted it with a pretend laugh.

There was nothing inside of him. Gina was gone. Gone again. Gone more than she had ever been gone. Someone had torn the curtains down and revealed there was nothing beyond—nothing outside, nothing worth anything. The world without Gina was unbearable.

He released his glass and swam, pulling his clothes off in the water and emerging naked just to make the others laugh. It was what was expected. Stephen always did what was expected of him, and he hated himself for it. He jumped in again to recover his clothes, and put them back on, despite the fact that they were leaden with river water.

Just before dawn, as the last of the partiers returned to their houses, Stephen stayed behind and stared up at the fading stars.

He flipped through the pictures on his phone again for a while.

It would be sunrise soon. Another day—but for what? All that he had worked for was suddenly stripped of meaning. Gina, Gina, Gina . . .

Why had he been permitted to go on living without her? If there was any goodness in the world, he should have been allowed to drop dead on the spot when she died.

He could always make up for that now.

He was aware that he was exhausted, and maybe a little drunk, but the idea got in and expanded, filling his mind. It would be easy enough to do. There was plenty of rope in the boathouse, and the beams were high. All it would take was the courage to see it through. Do it quick while he still held his bottle.

He admitted himself to the boathouse and switched on the

39

lights. It appeared to him now like the set of a play, not quite real, ready for the final act. He was dizzy, and his hands shook. Do it fast, do it fast. He tied a shoe to the end of a rope and used it as a weight to get it over the beam, then secured the end on the boat rack, testing a few times for the proper length. There was a leftover picnic chair outside that someone had swiped. He took this inside the boathouse and shut the doors. He looked up at his handiwork, as if this was one of the many projects he would be judged on. No points for a sloppy effort.

The act of mounting the chair and taking the rope was simply one of bluster, and then, with one final thought of Regina, he stepped up and kicked the back of the chair.

It was like lightning hit him.

He was hanging. Actually hanging.

And it was excruciating and his body was tingling and saying *no no no no no no*.

He was swallowed by an instant, unmistakable flood of panic and the certain knowledge that he'd made a mistake. His throat was being crushed, and there was a starburst of light and panic dancing before his eyes. The world was pulling him down and his head was pulling to the side. He grabbed for the rope, but the noose had slid and tightened. He tried to get his fingertips between his neck and the rope, but there was just no space. He dug in harder, clawing with his nails. His lower body jerked up at the knees

He did not want to do this. It had to stop. It had to.

Things started to go black, and while he wanted to fight, his body fought him and went heavier and limp and his fingers fumbled. And then . . .

He was standing. The pulling ceased.

The chair was there, under his feet. He almost fell off it in his scramble to balance on it, to stand long enough to rip the thing from his neck. He pulled the rope over his chin. The pain was intense, his neck bruised and battered and scraped all the way around. His whole body hurt from the weight and the strain and he shook so terribly he could barely keep upright. He jumped down, crashing almost immediately to his knees. The boathouse was throbbing and every vein in his body pulsed.

It had been stupid—more than stupid. Something more than stupid that existed outside the range of everything he understood. That idiotic thought from five minutes previously had almost cost him his life. He wanted to apologize to everyone who had ever died, and everyone who was alive. He wanted to apologize to the boats and the walls and the river and the rope. But all he could think to do was get down on the floor and rest on his back and breathe.

Breathing. Nothing was as good as breathing. How had he not noticed this?

"Are you all right?"

The voice was light, a little fearful, and coming from very nearby. Stephen pulled himself up to balance on his elbows, and found that there was a boy standing by his feet. It wasn't someone he knew.

"Are you all right?" the stranger said again.

He seemed to be maybe . . . maybe sixteen or so? He wore a thick brown sweater and spongebag trousers—an odd mix of clothes. His hair was dark blonde, neatly clipped and slicked down to his head in a severe side parting.

"I . . . I don't know . . ." Words were hard to find. "I'm sorry. I'm sorry."

Oh god, his throat hurt.

"You don't need to apologize to me," the boy said.

"Did you . . . the chair . . ."

"Yes," the boy said. "You seemed to want it."

Stephen coughed a laugh at that, and the pain this caused in his throat almost made him throw up. What had he done to his throat? There was a terrible ache now just along his jawline, and he reached up and winced instantly. The rope had cut and dug and broken all the skin.

"Can you sit up?" the boy asked.

"I think…" Stephen pushed himself up a bit and managed to get his back from the ground. He leaned over his bent knees and took a few deep breaths to try to steady his head.

"I can't believe I did that." His voice was a creaky whisper. "I can't believe I *actually did that*. How long . . ."

"Not terribly long. Less than ten seconds. You showed signs of regret at once."

Less than ten seconds? It had felt so much longer. Stephen rubbed at his jawline again, and was again rewarded with a zinging pain. The boy came and leaned against the boats next to him.

"Do I know you?" Stephen asked.

"I've been in this boathouse before, but you never noticed me, I suppose."

This was a confusing statement. Either this person was on the boats or he wasn't—and while there were many rowers at Eton, Stephen had probably seen and met them all at one time or another.

"I don't understand," Stephen said. "What's your name?"

"Peter."

"I'm Stephen."

"I know," Peter said.

Stephen blinked. Everything was still throbbing. Why did this strange person already know his name?

"Does it hurt?" Peter asked.

"A bit."

Stephen tested the skin again with the tips of his fingers. He didn't have to see it to know the damage would be very hard to hide.

"That will turn into quite the ugly blossom," Peter said. "But better a bruise than the alternative, eh?"

Stephen nodded. He wasn't in the mood to say much at the moment. It hurt to speak. Peter seemed to understand and came to sit by him. He was silent for a while, just looking at Stephen, then at the floor. It occurred to Stephen that he might have freaked Peter out and that it would probably be appropriate to say something.

"I hope I didn't . . . upset you." It sounded idiotic once it came out.

"Oh, no!" Peter said, almost cheerfully. "I was just worried for you. What made you do it?"

"My sister," he said. "She died. Three years ago."

"Oh. I'm sorry. What happened?"

"She took an overdose."

"Intentionally?"

"No. It was an accident."

"If you don't mind my asking . . . if it happened three years ago, why did you do this now?"

"I saw my family," Stephen said. "And it . . . it didn't go well."

"Ah, yes. Families. I certainly know how that can feel. And then you end up doing something rash. It appeared like you had just decided to do it on the spur of the moment."

So Peter had been watching the whole time? And did nothing to *stop* him? Had Stephen found someone preparing to hang himself, he would have either tried to talk him down, or tackled him, or yelled for help. Peter had done none of these things.

Also, Peter was odd-looking. Stephen couldn't put his finger on what was so strange. The clothes and hair were very retro—but that wasn't it. Maybe it was that he was so sickly pale, so calm, so . . .

Chipper.

There was something about Peter that didn't make sense.

"What you don't realize at the time is that you're not seeing the full picture," Peter went on. "You don't think about the fact that things will change. Things *always* change."

Stephen was just staring now, and Peter seemed to read his thoughts.

"You're wondering how I know. I know how you felt because I did it myself. Not quite the same way. I threw myself in the river. And all because of Simmons."

Stephen combed his brain for any Simmons he could think of but came up with nothing.

"Simmons? I don't think I know a Simmons."

"Oh, you wouldn't know Simmons. You'd remember him. The most beautiful boy in all the school, an absolute dish. He

44

sat next to me in Latin divs, and now I don't know more than twenty words of Latin. All of it, gone. For three years I said nothing, because . . . obviously, one couldn't. And one day, I really thought he knew. I was walking along the river, and he ran along to join me for no reason at all. The way he looked at me, the way he simply joined me . . . I thought he felt the same. And it was such a beautiful day, and no one was around, and there had been three years of longing. So, I kissed him. It did not go well. He turned and pushed me away and gave me a look that broke me into pieces. Then he ran off. It was all over. Everything. My life. He despised me, and he was going to tell, and nothing was worth living for, so I jumped into the river and let myself sink."

Stephen waited for the rest of the story, but it didn't seem to be forthcoming.

"So you . . ."

"Drowned," Peter said, matter-of-factly.

"But you got out . . ."

"They fished me out eventually, but I'd floated away a bit."

"You *drowned*," Stephen said. "And they had to revive you? How long were you in there?"

"Oh, they didn't revive me. I was long gone, I'm afraid."

Stephen shook his head in confusion.

"I'm dead," Peter said. "Have been for quite some time. I've been in this blasted boathouse for far too many years now. It was a stupid, stupid, stupid thing to do. I hate this boathouse. I didn't even row. And as it turns out, Simmons probably *did* feel the same way. I later saw him kissing Lockhart in this very room."

45

Stephen turned and painfully craned his sore neck to make sure he could see the rope behind him. Rope still in place. Chair standing up. It made no sense at all. He had definitely kicked the chair away, and the chair was definitely upright now, and he was on the ground, alive.

He must have gone too long without oxygen.

He lowered himself back down into a flat position on the floor and took some deep breaths. But when he looked up again, Peter was still there.

"It's so nice to have someone to talk to," Peter said. "Is this the first time you've ever seen anyone like me?"

He took Stephen's stunned silence as an answer.

"That's odd. There are certainly more of us around. Ghosts, I suppose you'd say."

"You're a ghost," Stephen repeated.

Stephen wasn't sure if it was good to engage with your own hallucinations, but still—any port in a storm.

"I'm wondering if the damage is permanent," Stephen said. "I think my brain has constructed you. I'm not quite sure why."

"It must be confusing for you, but I assure you, I am real. I died right here, in the river, all because of Simmons. You know, he came here once and stood on the spot where we kissed—or where I kissed him—and he stayed for quite a long time.

"I think he came here because he was sorry, but he had nothing to be sorry for. My father never came. He's in—he *was* in—the House of Lords. I presume he told everyone I died in a swimming accident. He would never admit his son threw himself in a river. That's not the kind of thing our family do."

This, Stephen understood completely. Had he actually

managed to hang himself, his parents' main priority would probably have been figuring out what to tell the neighbours and everyone at the club. Perhaps this very sad narrative was his brain trying to help him sort out what to do next.

"It would be wonderful to be alive now," Peter said. "I'd have led such a different life. I see what happens now. The romances that go on here, even in the open! I could even marry now! To *think* of it. When I think of all I missed . . . I'm sorry. I don't mean to turn the conversation to me. I've seen you. You've always seemed like a good sort to me. Quiet. Tall and stalwart and handsome, if you don't mind my saying. But certainly one of the good ones. It always *seemed* like you might have a story to tell and somewhere else you would rather be. I understand that feeling. I was always thinking about what it would be like away from here. It's all I want, really, to be away from here. If you could do anything right now, instead of being here, what would it be?"

Stephen hesitated.

"I'd like to go and be a policeman," he finally said.

"Ah." Peter waved his hand. "Go and be a policeman. I think you'd be a good one."

"You don't know me," Stephen said.

"I do. I told you, I've been in this bloody boathouse for ages. You always seemed all right to me. There's always a few who are all right, and you're one of them."

"Thanks," Stephen said. "And . . . you too."

"That's dashed kind of you," Peter said, looking away in what appeared to be embarrassment. "It's been a long time since a handsome boy had anything nice to say to me."

"You saved my life," Stephen said. "I don't know . . . you may be in my head, I don't know . . . but you saved my life."

"Oh, it was nothing, really. I just moved a chair."

The silence between them became a bit awkward.

"It's almost dawn," Peter said. "Look, I'll take this down. I'm not very strong, but I can handle a rope. All of this will be gone. You go and . . . you take care of yourself. Go on. I don't want to see you go, but it's for the best. Come on now."

Peter stood and gestured for Stephen to do the same.

"You're right," Stephen said. He pushed himself up slowly and opened one of the doors and saw the first show of sunlight taking over the sky, turning the night into something soft and violet-coloured and fresh-smelling. It really was like everything was new, and the gentle sound of the flowing river, the paddling ducks getting started for the day, the birds starting to sing in the trees . . .

He turned to see Peter clambouring up the side of the boats. Down came the rope a moment later, and there was Peter, climbing down with a cheer.

His life was his, and Gina would have thrown him in the river herself if she'd heard his insane plan. He could hear her yelling at him in his mind and the sound was sweet and the words were cutting: *Stephen, you utter tit. How does killing yourself help me? I love you, you fool. How did they make you so stupid?*

But Gina was not there. Only Peter, who was now folding the chair away.

"I'm going to go back now," Stephen said.

"Right then," Peter replied. "And I don't want to tell you what to do, but you really shouldn't do that again. Things

48

change. Never act as if situations won't change. You'll end up in a bloody boathouse forever. And . . ."

Stephen had a foot out the door.

"Yes?" he asked.

"I know you think I'm not real," Peter said. "But come back and see me, won't you?"

"I will," Stephen said. "I promise."

It wouldn't be long before Eton was awake, before someone saw the mark on his neck. As he walked back across one of the very spongy lawns, intentionally stepping off the path, Stephen both cursed and thanked the mark. Without it, he could have continued on and no one would have been any the wiser. But the mark was there to bring change. There was no outfit, no shirt, nothing that would cover it—nothing he could get away with wearing.

He didn't even try to go back into his building. Instead, he walked the high street, taking in the quiet, looking up at Windsor Castle from the end of the road, then walking back again. The first runners came out to pound the streets. They were too involved in their own running to look at Stephen closely. But as he got closer to home, Elliot Mogs, from his house, came out for his five-thirty morning run.

"Morning, Dene . . ." He stopped at once. "Your *neck*. What were you up to last night?"

"You don't want to know," Stephen said with a laugh.

It was Fourth of June, after all. Things happened. He could perhaps pretend it was a prank gone wrong.

The look on Mogs's face suggested not.

The san wouldn't open for a bit, though there were people there all the time, monitoring the sick bay. Stephen peered into the windows and saw other boys sleeping in the unit. He passed along until he found a nurse awake, sitting at a desk with a cup of tea, reading something on the internet. He knocked lightly on the window. This surprised her, but she came around and opened it up.

"I did this," he said, pointing at his neck.

The nurse looked, paused, inhaled softly through her nose.

"Is that a rope mark?"

"Yes."

"Did you do that to yourself?"

"Yes. Can I come inside?"

"I'll open the door," she said.

And she did so, then ushered him directly to one of the small examining rooms, where she sat him down.

"Was your intention to kill yourself, or was there some other purpose?" she said.

"It was my intention to kill myself, but I changed my mind."

The nurse nodded slowly.

"I see," she said. "I'm glad you changed your mind."

"Me too."

She nodded again, and her face was pinched in kindness.

"Your voice is quite rough. You may have injured your larynx. Does your throat hurt?"

"A bit," Stephen said.

"What's your name?"

"Stephen Dene."

"My name is Janet. Do you mind if I examine your neck,

Stephen, if I do it very gently?"

Stephen lifted his chin to make his throat more accessible, and the effort pulled painfully at the ripped-up skin. Janet was as gentle as she promised, feeling the wound all the way around, having him swallow, asking him to speak again. His voice was all gravel.

"I don't think this is too bad," she said. "The doctor might do an x-ray to see if there's any damage, but the bruising could be the worst of it. I think you changed your mind fairly quickly, didn't you?"

She looked into Stephen's face.

"Your eyes are a bit bloodshot," she added. "That will go away as well. All in all, I am very happy to see you in such good condition. Do you think you'd like a cup of tea?"

"Yes, please."

"Good. Come with me. We'll get it together."

Janet put her hand on his arm and guided him to the tiny kitchen used by the staff. Together, they went about the very ordinary process of putting bags into mugs and boiling the kettle. The tea felt a bit like acid going down his throat, but somehow, it was also good and reassuring.

"Stephen," she said, "the physical damage is likely not too serious. Obviously, the main concern is how you are feeling."

"I'm feeling much better, actually," he said. "It was stupid."

"I'm glad to hear it. You'll still need to be seen by the doctor, and it's very likely something will need to be done to help you. Do you agree that something needs to be done?"

"I agree."

"That's good. I'm going to call in Doctor Frankel, who is our resident psychiatrist. He's quite nice and very good at what he does. Everything you say will be absolutely confidential."

"But you need to put this in my record," he said. "I know everything stops here. They'll send me somewhere."

"You're not the first, Stephen. The pressures of this school . . ."

"I know I'm not the first."

Maybe it was the exhaustion finally hitting him, or the shock. Or maybe it was the fact that with the morning and the sun and the landing on the floor of the boathouse and taking that deep breath—Stephen was starting over. And there would be no lies, no covering up. No trying to fit within the system no matter the cost.

"I met one who succeeded," he said, setting down his tea. "In the boathouse. He helped me get down."

The nurse paused on this.

"Who . . . succeeded?"

"I realize how that sounds," he said. "And I don't know how it happened. But I met someone there who helped me, and he claimed to be dead. And that's why I'm alive. I imagine this will complicate things."

"Well," the nurse said, "the brain can do all sorts of things when deprived of oxygen. I'm going to phone Doctor Frankel at home. And I'll get you a cervical collar—one of those foam neck braces. It will cover up your neck and give you a bit of support. Then I'll have our assistant James walk back to your house with you, and you can get some things."

"I'm not going to do it again," Stephen said. "I stopped. I came here."

"I know," she said. "But it's best to have some company. It's all right, Stephen. You aren't alone in this."

"I know I'm not," he said. And for once, the morning sunlight felt hopeful, like something in him was finally lifting, something was finally free.

III

THE SPECIALIST

The hospital was outside Brighton. It was a sprawling building in some vague Victorian style, all arches and big windows, painted stark white. It was a seaside kind of building, and it reminded him of a massive vanilla ice-cream—one that had sixty-nine private patient rooms and three acres of highly manicured ground, including a path to the sea and a private beach. After being assessed, he was shown to a comfortable room, one without too much character—heavy curtains at the windows, a desk, a television mounted on the wall, everything in calm, muted colours. Judged by the decor, this could have been a roadside inn. There was already a daily schedule in a small plastic frame by his door.

Stephen was used to schedules and found himself studying it and making plans on how to get to each thing most efficiently, before he checked himself and reminded himself that he was in a hospital, not running across a town to try to get to a Latin div on time. The day was leisurely, but there was no room to sit and wallow. Breakfast at nine. A choice after that of either painting or taking a group bike ride (he'd do the bike ride), then one-on-one therapy, then lunch, then a "seaside walk", then group therapy, then a choice between yoga and tai chi (he'd do the tai chi), then time to write in his journal (which he now had to keep), and dinner. So this was what he would be doing for the rest of June, at least, while everyone else at school finished up. Provisions would be made, he was told, to help him secure his place at Cambridge and finish the Eton year somehow, but he didn't, he was assured, have to worry about that now.

He found that he wasn't worried about it at all. His room looked out at the sea, he didn't really mind speaking to the doctor, and the dinner wasn't that bad. He was here to get better, and the act of coming here was already a huge step.

His parents paid the bills but did not visit. This was absolutely expected and absolutely preferred.

The first few days passed in this way. Unsurprisingly, his doctor wanted to talk about Peter, but Stephen was hesitant. Regina—yes, he would finally discuss Regina. But something about Peter . . . it just wouldn't settle. He would replay their conversation in his head as he tried to get to sleep. It wasn't upsetting to think about Peter. On the contrary, it was reassuring. Hallucination or not, Peter was somehow—

His friend?

Fine. So he had an imaginary friend. But the doctor was more and more persistent each day, and each day, Stephen found himself becoming more and more reticent on the subject.

"This figure," the doctor would ask. "Did it speak or was it silent?"

"I know it wasn't there," Stephen would answer.

"But it did speak to you. What did it talk about?"

"About how this was a mistake."

"And what else?"

"Nothing else," Stephen would say.

And that was all he would give about Peter—no name, no details of the story he told. Let him remain a shimmering, faint vision in the eyes of the doctors.

After a week of this routine, Stephen found himself sitting in the library one evening, happily reading away when an orderly came in.

"The doctor would like to see you," he said. "Nothing's wrong, he just asked if you could pop in for a moment."

Stephen had just found himself in a comfortable place, reading in the summer evening sunlight. He wasn't thrilled about getting up to talk again. But he was trained to obey commands, so he got up and followed the orderly, down the now-shaded hall with its soft blue carpeting. It was rare to see a carpeted hospital, and Stephen was reminded that he was basically supported by a cushion of money.

His doctor was not alone. Next to him was a woman, maybe forty or so, with very dark black hair and skin. She wore a jolt of rose-coloured lipstick, highlighting the professionally polite smile all doctors seemed to have to wear at all times—the smile that bordered on a grimace. She was introduced as Doctor Marigold, and Stephen was informed that she would be taking over his care. Then they were left alone.

"I don't usually do sessions in the evening," Stephen said.

"I know," the woman said. "I'm sorry to disrupt your routine."

"Is there a reason my doctor has been changed?"

"I'm a specialist," she said. "And please, call me Felicia. I was hoping to speak to you a little bit more about what happened to you in the boathouse—specifically, with the boy you said you saw."

Stephen shifted uncomfortably.

"I'm told you don't like to talk about this," Felicia said.

"Am I so ill they had to bring in someone new?"

"No. If anything, the reports I'm reading are excellent. You're responding very well to treatment. You really just needed a chance to decompress. No—I'm here because, as you have probably realized by now, you experienced a neurological event. I am doing research on this very subject, and you'd be providing invaluable assistance to many other people if you would consent to participate in a test."

"What sort of test?" Stephen asked.

"A simple and painless one. It only takes a few hours. No pills, nothing physical. It's quick and simple. Not only would this test provide valuable data, I believe it would be of tremendous benefit to you."

"How?"

"Hallucinations are extremely common," she said. "Much more common than people realize. We're looking into what triggers certain types of hallucinations. We'd just check your brain function—and again, it's absolutely pain-free and simple. I think you'd like to know what happened, to know there's no lasting damage."

"Do you think there could be?" he asked.

"Based on what I've read of your case, I think your prognosis is excellent. And sometimes hallucinations are quite helpful. Quite pleasant. Which is why, sometimes, people don't want to share them. They're private."

She gave him a long, understanding look.

"I won't pry into what you saw," she said. "I merely want to check to see how your brain is functioning now. Would you be agreeable to that? It really would be a tremendous help."

Stephen didn't really feel like having his brain tested, but if it was helpful—well, he really had no excuse to say no.

"I suppose," he said.

"Very good. The facility is in London. We'd drive there and back this evening."

"This evening?" Stephen said. "Now?"

"Right now. My car is outside. I'll take you there, and you'll be back here in a few hours. We might be a little late, until midnight or so. Would that be all right?"

She was already on her feet, ushering him up and towards the door.

The sky was still heavy with sunlight when Stephen and Felicia walked to the car. These early-summer days really did seem to go on forever. Felicia, he noted, drove the same car as his father—a green Jaguar. Even the interior was the same. She said very little on the ride, which was fine by Stephen. He'd been given the cervical collar to carry and wear as he liked, and he put it on and used it like a travel pillow to drift off into a nap.

When he opened his eyes, they were driving through Knightsbridge. The streets were clogged with tourists taking pictures of anything and everything. The sky was just starting to dim in a great late-night sunset.

"Where are we going, exactly?" Stephen asked.

"Berkeley Square. Not far now."

"There's a hospital at Berkeley Square?"

"No. There is a house there. That's where we're doing our test."

They parked on the square, which was really a rectangle—a very tidy one, with a perfect green lawn. There were only a few people milling about there. The square itself was lined with flat-fronted Georgian houses, most of which looked to be occupied by businesses, and therefore, mostly unoccupied at this hour.

"This one," Felicia said, pointing to a four-storey house with a slate-grey front. She unlocked the door and they stepped inside. Stephen was hit by a familiar and quite pleasant smell—books. Lots of them. Funny how books could end up giving off such a scent, however subtle.

The reception area was a long, narrow room halved by a staircase. The rest of the space was crowded by bookshelves precisely filled with what looked like old volumes, all in good condition, many behind glass. There were two rooms radiating off the reception area from either side and these, too, seemed to be full of books. By the staircase there was a very fine and elegant desk with a green-shaded lamp. Just behind this stood a grim-faced woman of about fifty, with a steely crew-cut. She wore a loose, square-collared blouse and a voluminous pair of trousers, both of which were in muted colours.

"Hello, Stephen," she said. "Welcome."

"Hello," Stephen replied.

Felicia looked a little confused by this exchange, as if saying hello wasn't quite something from her world.

"This is a bookshop," Felicia said.

"I guessed that."

"It's a very good bookshop," she clarified.

Stephen gave her a side glance.

"Why are we in a bookshop?" he asked.

"This is a technique called 'flooding'," she said. "It's usually used in the treatment of phobias and compulsions. The idea is that we quickly and safely immerse you in a situation in order to free you of fears."

"I'm not afraid of bookshops," he said.

"This is not a case of phobia. I just want you to go upstairs and look in every room of this house. And take this. It's dark."

She removed a torch from her purse and handed it to him.

"You want me to just . . . go upstairs? And this is going to help me?"

"It is," she said.

The woman with the steely hair folded her arms over her chest and looked on. When Stephen glanced her way again, she gave him a solemn nod, which he supposed was meant to encourage, or to tell him to get on with it.

"Right," he said, sighing loudly and not caring that the doubt in his voice was audible. He flicked on the torch, and it spilled a very weak light. He looked to Felicia again, wondered what the hell kind of clinic he'd been sent to, then proceeded to climb the steps. The steps were carpeted with a roll of oriental red, with metal bars pinching the carpet back at the folds to keep it from coming loose. They had a mellow creak as befitted such a bookshop, which Stephen could now see specialized in antique and rare books. Prints of Georgian scenes and ducks and hunting dogs lined the steps to the second floor, which was still veiled in darkness.

"Wouldn't it just be easier to turn on the lights?" Stephen called down.

"Try along the wall," Felicia called up.

"Try along the wall," he murmured under his breath. He did so, feeling along, reaching into the spaces between the bookcases. There was some light coming in, the remnants of the sunset, which was now nearly at ten. But there was only the one window at the far end of this floor, so it really was quite dark up there. When he did find the light switch, nothing happened.

"It's not working," he said.

"Just use the torch," Felicia called.

Stephen switched on the torch and shone it around. Books, chairs, bookcases. He peered into the rooms and saw more of the same.

"Now what?" he called down.

"Up to the top, please."

Stephen sighed and began to climb again. The third floor was much the same as the second. As he turned to climb the stairs to the fourth floor, he stopped involuntarily. There was a smell of . . .

Was it fire? Not fire in a fireplace, but fire as in things that should not be burning, acrid and sour. He turned around, then looked up. When he moved, the smell simply went away. It had gone from overwhelming to non-existent in seconds.

He climbed a few more steps and hit the smell again, and again, it went away. Up again. This floor, though not structurally different than the other three, was more shaded. There were heavy curtains on the window at the top of the stairwell and they were drawn. The walls were papered on this floor, a messy flocked pattern that seemed different from the tasteful schemes of the lower floors. It felt cold. It felt . . .

It felt wet, actually. Stephen drew his hand away and touched the tips of his fingers together, but there was no moisture there. He touched the wall again. Definitely wet. And yet again, his hand was dry.

He was being an idiot. There were many good reasons why dry walls might feel wet. Silk papering, for example, or a paper with a metallic sheen. They might both feel cool or wet to the touch. Maybe this entire exercise was to show him how suggestible he really was, and how you could reason your way out of a situation.

The top floor seemed to be almost entirely disused. There were crates of books around, mostly right at the top of the stairwell, as if someone had only been willing to climb so far, then simply threw them down. The doors to the rooms were closed. It was surprisingly cold given the fact that it was the top floor and a boiling hot day. If anything, this floor should have been unbearable and muggy. Something in him strongly suggested turning around and going back downstairs. This floor was creepy. Simple and plain. Creepy. Unpleasant.

He was not going to be creeped out by a dark hall with some boxes in it and some weird wallpaper that felt wet. He was still an Etonian—he was still *himself*—and Stephen was not the kind of person who simply gave up if something was a little weird or unpleasant. He walked to the first door and opened it. The room was small and cramped and looked to have been an old servant's bedroom. It was filled with folded-up cardboard boxes and split books and a few chairs with shredded stuffing.

Second room—larger, with an adjoining door to the first. This appeared to be maybe an old bedroom, with a fireplace on the joining wall and a shared chimney. The room was papered in a delicate pink pattern which looked both old and fresh. There were scorch marks around the fireplace. And aside from more boxes and an old metal bedframe, this room contained nothing.

The third door faced the square. This one actually contained some light. The paper was yellow. The chairs were wooden and broken. No boxes. The entire floor was wasted space. He'd now gone everywhere there was to go and was embarrassed by his unease. If this was a test to make you feel like a knob, then he had exceeded expectations.

"I've looked everywhere," he said, turning around to leave. "And there's no—"

There was a little girl in the hall, directly in his path, just a few feet away. She was about four, maybe, with brown hair. She held the rail of the steps with one hand and a doll in the other. Where she had come from, he had no idea. He'd heard nothing, and only seconds had passed.

He felt a tickle in his chest.

"Hello," he said.

"Hello," the girl replied.

What the hell kind of a test was this?

"There's a . . . child up here," he yelled. "Should I . . . bring her down with me?"

No one responded below.

"Did you hear me?" he called again.

The child plucked at her doll's hair, pinching clump after clump.

"What's your name?" the girl asked. "I'm Alexandria."

"I'm Stephen."

"Hello, Stephen. This is my house."

Something about this girl was not right. Her clothes, for example, were like nothing he'd ever seen. And he knew people who shopped at some very exclusive boutiques and dressed their kids up in all kinds of exotic and adorable outfits. This seemed to be a kind of . . . pinafore? Was that the word he wanted? A little pink dress with what looked like an apron sewn onto the front?

"There's a chip in my doll's face," she said, holding up the doll. There was indeed a small chip missing from its stark white cheek, right next to the eye.

"I'm sure it can be fixed," he said. Not that he had any idea whether or not that was acually true.

He looked around for any signs of cameras. Maybe someone in a lab somewhere was collecting data on his startle reflex? Something? Someone in a lab was likely laughing their ass off.

"Not many people talk to me," the girl said. "They get afraid of me."

"They do?"

"I do get angry sometimes."

She hung her head shyly again.

Even if this girl was—as he had decided—some kind of

plant, she was still a small child and her lines didn't seem rehearsed. So he had serious questions about who might let their little girl sit around in creepy old bookshops at night to freak out people who had recently been admitted to mental health facilities.

This was a test. Stephen understood tests. He passed tests. He had to continue.

"Why would anyone be afraid of you?" he asked.

"Because I threw Andy into the fire."

"Your doll?"

"My brother."

"You threw your brother into the fire?" he asked.

She nodded again.

"He was little," she explained. "And he made a lot of noise. So I put him in the fire. Everyone was angry."

Stephen felt his muscles freezing up—hands first, then his arms, then a locking in the legs, rendering him unable to move.

"He didn't make a noise after that," she said, pulling on the doll's hair some more. "But everything smelled bad. Mummy was very angry. She held my head under the water in the bath."

The steel-haired woman was suddenly in view, standing at the end of the hall. Her sudden appearance caused Stephen to jump and his heart to race around a bit. She also hadn't made a sound.

"Stephen," she said, "that torch you have with you. Keep it switched on, and touch the child with it."

"What?"

"Just do as I say. Gentle now. Keep it on, and touch the girl with it."

65

The little girl looked up at Stephen curiously. Stephen looked once again for the cameras, but he would never find them. You could hide a camera in anything.

"Stephen," the woman said, with a firm voice, "I realize this is an odd instruction, but follow it. Simply touch the child with the torch."

Stephen felt a wall of refusal building inside of him. He didn't like the way he was being treated, or the child was being treated—both of them creeping around in a bookstore like two unwilling players in a piece of crap performance art.

"No," he said.

"Why not?"

"What's happening, Stephen?" the girl asked.

"I have no idea," Stephen replied. He moved to put his arm around her in protection, but when he did so, something felt wrong. He looked down to see that about one-quarter of his hand appeared to be inside of Alexandria's arm.

"Stephen," the woman said again. "Do it."

He checked again. Hand, definitely sticking into the arm. He pulled his fingers back quickly.

A projection, surely. This was all a trick, and it had to end. He pushed the torch in Alexandria's direction, and the moment it made contact, her eyes went wide and she seemed to let out a silent scream . . .

. . . or something. Because then there was a light, bright, white, flooding the hallway and blinding him for a moment. Then there was a rush of air, like a massive industrial fan—or a dozen massive industrial fans had all gone on at once. Then the rush stopped, and there was a strange, new smell in the air, vaguely floral, and vaguely like a wood-burning fire—but really neither one adequately described it.

When his eyes adjusted again, the steely woman was gone. As was Alexandria.

Stephen got up quickly and leaned over the rail.

"What the hell was that?" he called. He hurried down the steps, two at a time. Felicia was waiting for him downstairs with an expression of polite interest.

"What . . ." Stephen pointed up at the ceiling. "Just . . . what?"

"Why don't you sit," Felicia said, pointing at a chair. "Talk to me about what just happened."

"*What just happened*? Is this some kind of Derren Brown thing or—"

"Stephen," she said, "calm down. Sit. Talk to me. Tell me exactly what you saw."

Stephen did not sit. He paced from the chair to the glass-fronted bookcase.

"You sent me to talk to some *child* who said she threw her brother in a fire," Stephen said, his voice rising to a yell. "And then she said her mum drowned her in a bath. And then that woman said to touch the girl with the torch, as if that isn't creepy. And then the girl isn't even there. What is she? How did you project—"

"There is no projection."

"Or reflection, whatever. Some trick with glass and light. What the hell is this supposed to be?"

"It's not a trick," Felicia said calmly.

"I should report you," Stephen said, pointing his finger.

"Report me for what?"

"This can't be ethical, what you're doing. Are you even a doctor?"

"No," she said.

He hadn't really expected to be right on that one, and it stopped him.

"What's going on?" he said. "Who are you?"

He noticed he sounded more calm, but he was anything but.

"You're now standing in what many people consider to be the most haunted building in London," Felicia said. "Aside from the Tower."

"You're telling me that you brought me here because this building is full of *ghosts*? That's what this is about?"

"These things are hard to measure," Felicia replied. "We have to rely on anecdotal evidence, but there's quite a lot about this place. Eight people have been reported to have gone mad with fright after staying upstairs, and three have reportedly died."

Stephen laughed—a dark, unhappy laugh—and put his head in his hands.

"Stephen, listen to me," she said. "The world is more complicated than you know. You're rational. As am I. Most ghost *sightings* are not real. But that is not the same thing as saying ghosts are not real. Many supposed ghost sightings are the products of suggestion—the mind's desire to find patterns in randomness, so shapes are seen in shadows, ordinary noises become whispering voices, the cold breeze from under the door becomes a spectral presence. That's all well understood. Actual ghosts—"

"No," Stephen said, shaking his head. "No."

"Please let me finish. Actual ghosts are . . . well, we don't

68

know precisely, but they appear to be a malfunction of some kind. Leftover energy that does not disperse quite as it should."

"Take me back to the hospital," Stephen said.

"Let me finish. There is a reason there are so many stories. There is a reason the stories go back through so much of history. We understand very little about it, but here is what we do know—people who truly can see ghosts develop the ability after a close brush with death. Also, this event—whatever it is—needs to take place between the ages of fourteen and eighteen or so. There can be slight variations, depending on individual brain chemistry, but that's generally how it works. We don't have enough data to know if it runs in families."

"Fine," Stephen said, raising his hands. "I'll go myself."

He went to the door, only to find it locked. He shook it once, then turned back to Felicia.

"This has to be illegal now," he said. "Open this door. I signed myself into the hospital, but I never agreed to be locked in."

"We're not in the hospital."

"Which means this is tantamount to false imprisonment, most likely. I'll break the pane if you don't open it right now."

Felicia didn't move, so Stephen grabbed an iron doorstop from the ground and lifted it.

"You have a valuable ability," she said. "You could serve your country."

She joined him at the door and pointed to a car idling at the kerbside, maybe twenty yards away. It was a prim and anonymous-looking black Mercedes.

"The driver of that car is instructed to take you to Thames House," she said. "Do you know what Thames House is?"

"You're talking about the headquarters of MI5?"

"I am. There is someone there who wishes to speak with you. Listen to what he has to say."

"Now you're telling me I'm going to go talk to some *spies*," he said.

"Security services, not spies, necessarily. The very location should give you some confidence that this is no prank. Just go, listen, and then you'll be returned to the hospital."

"You're not coming?"

"No," she said. "I will not be coming. My role in this is over."

"And if I wanted to go back now?"

"Then the car would take you. But you'd wonder forever about what they wanted to say to you at MI5."

Annoyingly, she was right.

"What about the torch?" he asked, holding it up. "Explain this."

She took the torch from him.

"Go and get in the car," she said.

She wasn't lying.

The car cruised down to the Embankment Road, turning by Westminster Bridge and heading along to Vauxhall, stopping in front of the massive structure that was Thames House. Stephen had read enough and seen enough to know the building by sight. The driver said nothing at all for the entire trip, and continued to say nothing now that they had stopped. Stephen let himself out, and immediately saw that there was a man sitting on the wide steps leading up to the grand arch that fronted the building. He had very striking white hair, which

70

didn't quite match his face, which was young and clean shaven. He wore an elegantly tailored but nondescript grey suit—a light summer one that didn't crumple in the heat.

"Stephen Dene," the man said, standing and extending his hand. "I expect you've had rather a strange evening."

The matter-of-factness of the man's voice was soothing.

"I'm Thorpe," the man said. "Come inside. Unless you want to walk. It's nicer out here than in there, but it's your choice."

Part of Stephen wanted to go inside, just to be assured that this man *could* go inside. But a bigger part believed him, and preferred the cooling night air and being able to walk. Also, he could simply run off if he chose to do so.

"Outside," he said.

"All right. Let's walk a bit."

The stretch of the river along Vauxhall was darker than the path further up, and the bushes rattled a bit as they passed. Rats? Drunks? It was hard to tell.

"I've read your records," Thorpe said. "Quite impressive."

Stephen had no reply to that. That was simply what people said to you when you went to Eton, that you were impressive.

"We've come to recruit you," Thorpe said.

"Recruit me for *what*?"

"To restart a group that hasn't been functional since the early 1990s. It appears that London is a city plagued by the departed. This causes any number of problems, anything from disruptions on Tube lines to accidents or even death. So, for years, we had a group who could see and deal with these issues. It's not something we really want getting out—that we run a unit that deals with ghosts. And, as I said, the last unit was disbanded some time ago. But it's been decided that it must be reopened. And we'd like you to be at the head of it."

"Me? How did you even *find* me?"

"We've been looking for someone like you for a long time. We had feelers out at hospitals and clinics. We were looking for someone around your age, someone who had just had a close brush with death, someone who then reported seeing . . ."

". . . ghosts."

"Ghosts, yes. When you turned up, we acted quickly. You have everything we're looking for—a fine academic record, high-scoring, rational, good levels of physical fitness, and some experience in leadership. Eton certainly trains for that."

"And you want me to run a group?" Stephen said. "What kind of group?"

"Technically, a police unit. Much of the work is done under the auspices of other professions, to allow access to various places. So you could be uniformed police, or work for the Underground, or British Gas…"

"A police officer?" Stephen said, stopping him. "I could become a *police officer*?"

"Yes. Does that interest you?"

It definitely interested him, but it still all felt like a trick.

"What was the business with the torch?" Stephen asked.

Thorpe reached his hand into his pocket and produced a plastic vial. He illuminated his palm with his phone, revealing that the vial contained two small, clear stones.

"These are diamonds," he said. "Not particularly valuable ones. They're small and flawed. There is a third one of this set, which is located in the torch you handled earlier. When a current is

72

run through these stones, they produce something—I'm not going to pretend to know what—but something that dismisses whatever the thing . . . the . . . ghost."

"You're joking," Stephen said.

"Trust me, I wish I was. I'm not necessarily any more comfortable with this than you are. But it is what it is."

"You're saying that you have *diamonds* that can get rid of ghosts."

"That is exactly what I am saying, because it's what I've been told. Diamonds are excellent semiconductors. They're pure carbon. I don't know why they work. I don't know where we got them. But we have them. They are quite a precious resource. They're called *termini*. Each one, a terminus. An end point. Name's a bit on the nose, but I suppose it does provide an accurate description."

Stephen rubbed at his forehead. The day had been far too long.

"You would be in charge of the immediate workings of the group," Thorpe said. "You'd have to be, as I can't do what you do. But I would be your supervisor within MI5. I'd help you get access to recourses."

Stephen went to the balustrade and took a few deep breaths of Thames breeze, with its peculiar odour of salty ocean and rubbish. If this was a trick, who was playing it? To what end?

What if it was all true?

There had to be a way to know. And then it hit him.

"I want proof," Stephen said.

"What kind of proof?"

"I need to access records from Eton," Stephen said. "All files on students coming in . . ."

Best to give a range, not allow for any clues as to what he had seen. He had no idea what year Peter had entered the school, but twentieth century seemed a good enough window to start with. He certainly wasn't from a recent time.

"Everyone entering between 1900 and 1970. Complete files."

"And this would assure you that what you saw was real?"

"I want to see those files," Stephen said.

"It would be quite a lot of files."

"I don't care."

Thorpe nodded.

"I'll see what I can do. Until then . . . the car will return you to the hospital. I will be in touch."

Stephen woke up the next morning to the sound of knocking, the sun pouring on to his bed from the curtains he'd forgotten to close the night before. A nurse carefully opened his door.

"Mr. Dene? Stephen? Are you awake?"

She put a new schedule in the frame by the door. The same round as before, with the usual variations. Today he had a choice between kite flying and learning about the spices that go into various curries of the world. He rubbed his eyes, wondered what the hell he had been doing the night before. He was in a hospital, and hours before he had been taking out a child ghost and meeting with MI5.

He decided to go with the kite flying, and left his room in a daze. He ate a not-at-all-bad full English in a daze, looking around at his fellow patients. As he was leaving to go to the first therapy session of the day, a nurse approached.

"Something for you," she said. "I was told to give it to you and tell you that you should probably go back to your room to open it. Your first session has been moved by an hour."

She looked puzzled, even slightly disturbed, as if this was not something that usually happened and therefore could not possibly be good. She handed him a large padded envelope that contained a flat, rectangular object. A tablet computer, from the feel of it.

He returned to his room and shut the door. The envelope did, indeed, contain a tablet computer. It had no password to unlock. There was only one icon on the home screen, and it was of a folder labelled REQUESTED FILES. When Stephen clicked this, he found a long string of sub-folders, each one labelled with a year, 1900–1970, just as he had asked.

"You did that fast," Stephen said to himself.

Someone had spent a lot of time doing this. It appeared that every single page had been hand-scanned, then organized. The names were alphabetized by last name, and he had no idea what Peter's last name was, but searched the name.

A lot of Peters entered Eton in the twentieth century.

But he had another name—Simmons. Once he entered that, it limited the results to sixteen yearly files. He scanned these, reading the file for every Peter he found. The files contained home information, information on parents, divs taken and marks scored. It was all very familiar.

It took an hour, but he finally found something on his fifteenth Peter. *Maxwell Lemington Addison, Peter Edward (Hon.)*. Entered Eton 1946, but his file ended in 1949.

Three years, Peter had said. Three years of looking at

Simmons. And there was a Simmons in the 1946 class. Stephen flicked through the pages of divs and grades and notes on Peter, finally coming to Lent term, 1949, where the record stopped abruptly and was replaced with a single typewritten page. The scan captured something of the tone of the event—the official Eton stationery of the time, the red looking rusty from age and the blue slightly dusty. The paper itself had browned just a bit. And the text was typed in the centre of the page, very deliberately, very terse. The typewritten letters were just a bit uneven, as if they couldn't quite get out the words:

```
Student deceased following accident on river,
6th May. All further records located at Eton
Police Station.
```

Stephen set the tablet down on his bed and looked out at the sunny day and the distant view of the sea just over the trees. Someone was kite-surfing with a bright rainbow-striped kite. He touched the glass of the window, and it was warm under his fingers. Such a thin piece of glass separated in from out.

Peter was real. The girl, real.

All of it was real.

Thorpe came for visiting hours the next day, while Stephen was taking an agonizingly slow group seaside walk. He had been eyeing the sea, longing to run in and swim for miles. He missed his swimming and rowing and feeling the water, and it seemed like a good, normal thing to feel.

Thorpe met him outside, and they walked around a deserted

part of the gardens.

"Did you find what you needed?" Thorpe asked.

"How exactly would this work?" Stephen said. There was no need to answer directly and verify or deny anything.

"You'd be moved to London, where I'd brief and train you for four weeks. From there, you'd go to the police academy at Hendon for formal training. Between that and a few other courses we want you to go on, you'd be training continuously for eight months."

"And after that?"

"And after that, we assess. And if all has gone to plan, you begin work and start to build your team."

"Build it how?"

"Find more people like yourself. We'll help you locate them. There's a lot to learn, but you're more than up to the task. Do you agree?"

"Do you believe this?" Stephen said. "Do you think this is real?"

"My belief doesn't come into it."

"But do you?" Stephen asked.

Thorpe paused and considered his reply.

"I believe what I've heard on good authority," he said. "Frankly, in the work I do, you learn to expand the bounds of your credulity. The world is an odd place. I don't know what I would do in your shoes, but I can tell you the offer is absolutely legitimate. The question is—do you want to go back from where you came, finish up the year, go to Cambridge, or would you like to see what all this could mean? It's an offer that will only be made once. What is your answer?"

There was really only one answer to give.

"When do I go?"

"Now, if you'd like. The doctors here feel you're fine to leave. We have someone in London you can follow up with. You'll have a flat. It's nothing too fancy, but very well-located. For this first part, you'll be with me, working at Thames House."

"And my family?" Stephen said. "What will they be told?"

"The hospital will inform them that you've discharged yourself."

"What do I tell them after that?" Stephen asked.

"Whatever you want, aside from the truth. I'd suggest you simply tell them you are joining the police."

The sun came out from behind the clouds, as if on cue.

"In that case," Stephen said, resisting the urge to smile, "I'm going to need my phone."

IV

THE BOY IN THE SMOKE

It was a typical December day in London—dark, vaguely rainy. Constable Stephen Dene walked quickly, head down, through the confused crowds clinging to the outer regions of Harrods, all of them moving in confused, pointless patterns with their green signature Harrods bags. The lights that outlined the building were already illuminated, even through it was only two o'clock.

The uniform was fairly warm and comfortable. It was still new and despite two ironings still had some of the creases from the packages it had come in. Still, it was the best outfit he had ever worn. Once it was on, he felt different. He felt right. People stopped him and asked for directions and help and occasionally, for photos. Some people his own age sneered at him, and most people seemed a bit confused by his youth.

The training had been intense, but as Thorpe had pointed out, Eton did nothing if not prepare one for intense training.

For six months, he had done nothing but study, train and practise. He was moved around a lot so no one really got to know him for long. One day, Thorpe just told him it was done. He was given the uniform, the identification, the car, access to the databases—all the keys to the kingdom. It was time to build the team. He was to look for people his age or younger who had recently had accidents and claimed to see people that weren't there. He was to put feelers out at A&Es around the city.

But there were two things to do first.

The police database, he was amused to find, was called HOLMES—the Home Office Large Major Enquiry System—a somewhat redundant name that had been made to fit the acronym. The information he needed wasn't on this, so he had to look through several sub-systems until he got the address he was looking for. It had happened in Knightsbridge, in some maisonette round the corner from Harrods. The flat had since changed hands and was now owned by a couple based in Dubai.

Stephen rounded the corner and checked his notes. Number seventeen. That was the one he wanted. It looked like every other building on the street—gold and red brick, expensive, quiet. The flat was the one on the third floor. The lights were off. With his uniform and new abilities, it would be easy to get into the building and get the door opened. The flat was likely vacant.

But he found he couldn't quite move. He stood looking up at it for a very long time.

"No one's there," said a voice behind him.

Stephen turned to see the woman from the bookshop, the

one with the steel-grey hair. Her clothes were the same. Every single thing about her was the same—washed out, grey, almost blending into the December sky and the pavement.

"I thought you might turn up here," she said.

"Who are you?" he asked.

"That's not something you need to know. But I think you know *what* I am."

"Why were you there in the bookstore that night?"

"Also not necessary for you to know. But I think I know why you've come here. You're looking for your sister."

Stephen turned back to the dark window.

"Who becomes a ghost?" he asked. "Is she here?"

"Though related, those are two different questions." The woman folded her arms over her chest and looked up at the building. It appeared as though she would offer no more information, but then she opened her mouth again.

"It's not that common," she said. "Those of us who are lucky or unlucky enough to achieve this status . . . we're a rather select group."

"Is it because you have some unfinished business, or—"

"What utter rot!" She laughed a laugh that was somewhere between a cough and a roar. "Unfinished business. Whatever do you read? No one knows why. Something just goes wrong. It's not meant to be this way. It's like being stuck in a doorway, never being able to go in or out, unless someone helps you along."

"With this."

He took the device from his pocket. He had wired one of the stones into a phone, which was much easier to carry and less obvious to use than a torch.

"That looks a more sensible casing," she said. "I told them you had good sense."

"So if you know about the terminus, why don't you have someone use it on you?"

"Because I have a duty," she said. "I arrived here by accident but remain by choice. And you, my boy, have a duty as well. That tool you have is a serious business. You must use it with care."

"My sister," he said.

It wasn't a question, but she understood.

"Your sister is not here. She did not return."

"How do you—"

"Stephen, ask yourself the merits of that question. I am in a position to know. And you should be happy with this news. Your sister is not stuck. She is gone. You are not going to be forced to make the decision of whether or not you should use that device."

He gripped the phone. A siren went off in the distance. Stephen could imagine the ambulance that had come here, the one that had been called so many hours too late . . .

"Let me impart one piece of advice, Mr. Dene." The woman's usually stern voice had taken on a somewhat softer tone. "Do not go looking for the dead. You'll be seeing enough without going and looking for people who are probably not there. There's nothing in this place for you but heartache, and I won't let you stand here and wallow when there are things to be done."

There was just enough authority in her voice for Stephen to understand that this was an order, and it came from a place of real power.

"There's one more thing I have to do," he said.

"Yes," she replied. "I thought there might be. That one I understand, but no more. No more."

He drove to Eton that very evening, waiting only for the evening to come and the traffic to clear. He parked at Windsor for a bit and wandered around in the cold drinking a coffee, working up the nerve to cross the river. Term was safely over—only the beaks and masters would still be around, and many of them would have left for the holiday as well. He was well-bundled in a black coat and hat and scarf. Going in uniform would have drawn attention.

He left the car in Windsor and walked over the bridge. There was smoke drifting over the water, a floating hint of a bonfire somewhere in the distance. The air smelled strongly of it. The day was grey and heavy, the frosty air cutting into his exposed skin.

He wondered how he would be when he got past the vast new boating centre and to the old boathouse. Would he shake or start crying? Would everything come back? His steps were steady, though. His heart rate was maybe a little quick, but nothing more.

And he didn't even have to use the key in his pocket, the one he'd walked away with in June. Peter was sitting on the dock, looking at a cluster of ducks swimming in a circle. He didn't turn, even when Stephen was almost on top of him.

"Peter?"

This got a jolt of a response.

"Stephen!" Peter jumped to his feet, all smiles. He looked

like he was about to reach out, then he backed up nervously, moving from foot to foot before sinking his hands into the pockets of his trousers. "You came back!"

"I did. Can I sit with you? Talk a bit?"

"Of course! Of course! You can stay as long as you like! I've been thinking of you. I always hoped you were doing well. And you look well!"

"I'm good," Stephen said, sitting down on the cold boards of the dock. "Surprisingly so."

Peter sat back down, cross-legged, facing Stephen directly.

"Well, I'm glad to hear it. Did you go to university?"

"In the end, no," Stephen said. "I'm a police officer now."

"You're not! You said that's what you wanted to do! What's it like, being a police officer? Do you get your hat stolen a lot?"

Stephen shook his head.

"I'm not really a . . . normal police officer. I have a special job. That's partly what I want to talk to you about."

Stephen looked around to make sure they were entirely alone.

"Gosh," Peter said. "Sounds secret."

"It is, a bit. It's a lot to explain, but . . . there is a police force that deals with . . . well, people like you."

"You're not serious," Peter said.

Stephen put his hand on the phone in his pocket.

"I have a device," he said. "If I used it on you, you would . . . leave."

Peter stared at him dumbly, and the ducks, sensing weirdness, hustle-swam away from them.

"I won't . . ." Stephen said quickly. "I didn't come to . . . I

84

thought you'd want to know, and I promised . . ."

"Does it hurt?" Peter asked.

"I don't know," Stephen said. "But probably not. That's what I've been told. I've used it once. It's quick."

"And where do I go?"

"I don't know," Stephen said. "But you move on, away from here."

"Which is something," Peter said. "Freedom by any means."

"Freedom by any means," Stephen repeated.

"And you can do this?"

"I can," Stephen said.

Peter looked out over the river. He seemed to blend into the smoke.

"I always thought a handsome boy would come back and save me," he said, smiling a little. "That's how fairy tales end."

"I don't know that this is much of a fairy tale," Stephen said.

"It is for me."

He reached out and took Stephen's hand. Peter felt more solid than the girl, but cold.

"I'd like to go," Peter said. "I'd like to get away from this blasted place. I'd like it if you did that for me, Stephen."

Stephen nodded and took a deep breath.

"Now?"

"Now is as good a time as any. You'll stay for the whole thing?"

"It's very quick," Stephen said again.

He removed the phone. It was an old model he'd picked up online for close to nothing. It had actual touch-buttons, not a screen, and an old battery that could be easily gutted. He'd cleaned out the insides and taped in the terminus, a lithium battery, and wired it all together. All he had to do was push 1 and 9 at the same time to complete the circuit.

Peter nodded a bit nervously, looked down, then got to his knees and gave Stephen a kiss on the cheek. Then he sat down again quickly.

"Thank you," he said. "Now, Stephen, please."

Stephen's hand was shaking. This was different from the girl. Different, but . . .

But right.

Peter closed his eyes. Stephen held out the phone, pressing it into Peter's hand. It had to touch, that was the only rule. You had to make contact.

"Thank you," Stephen said. "For saving me."

Then he pushed the buttons.

WORLD BOOK DAY
6 MARCH 2014

WORLD B**OO**K DAY *fest*

Want to **READ** more?

 your LOCAL BOOKSHOP

- Get some great recommendations for what to read next

- Meet your favourite authors & illustrators at brilliant events

- Discover books you never even knew existed!

 WWW.BOOKSELLERS.ORG.UK/ BOOKSHOPSEARCH

 your LOCAL LIBRARY

You can browse and borrow from a HUGE selection of books and get recommendations of what to read next from expert librarians—all for FREE! You can also discover libraries' wonderful children's and family reading activities.

 WWW.FINDALIBRARY.CO.UK

 Visit **WWW.WORLDBOOKDAY.COM** to discover a whole *new* world of books!

- Downloads and activities
- Cool games, trailers and videos
- Author events in your area
- News, competitions and new books —all in a **FREE** monthly email

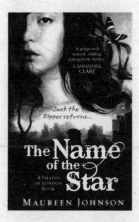

Suite Scarlett

Hilarious romantic
comedies set in a
famous art deco hotel
in New York City

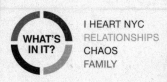